Saint Inn of Alaska

Apostle and Missionary

by Sarah Elizabeth Cowie

Conciliar Press
Ben Lomond, California

SAINT INNOCENT:
Apostle and Missionary

Illustrations courtesy of Saint Herman of Alaska Press

Published by   Conciliar Press
                     P.O. Box 76
                     Ben Lomond, California 95005-0076

Printed in the United States of America

ISBN 1-888212-74-8

Manufactured under the direction of Double Eagle Industries.
For manufacturing details, call 888-824-4344
or e-mail to info@publishingquest.com

Introduction

IF YOU CLOSE YOUR EYES and think about Alaska, what do you see? Eskimos and igloos? Mountains of snow? Polar bears and icebergs? Do you know that not all Alaskan natives are Eskimos? There are many different tribes of native peoples. Each has its own language and way of life.

Many of these native peoples have been Orthodox Christians for over two hundred years. This is largely due to the missionary efforts of one man, Saint Innocent of Alaska. He converted and baptized thousands of native people into the Christian faith. He was a wonderful and godly man who lived a missionary life full of adventures that you would never dream of! Many people believe he is the greatest Christian missionary of all time.

1

The Early Years

SAINT INNOCENT WAS BORN on August 26, 1797, in the village of Anga in southern Siberia, which was part of the Russian Empire. (This was long before there were cars, electricity, or even radios.) His parents were Eusebius and Thekla Popov. They loved God very much, went to all the church services, and were careful to live as Christians should, with kindness and love. Eusebius Popov was the sacristan in the village church. That means he took care of the vestments, as well as everything used in the altar.

Saint Innocent was their first child. His parents named him John, after Saint John the Faster, Patriarch of

1797.
On August 26, John Popov is born in Anga Village, Irkutsk province. His godparents, Savva and Justina, bear witness to his baptism.

Constantinople. Eusebius and Thekla were joyous and thankful that God had given them a son. He was baptized as a little baby by the village priest in the Saint Elias Church.

In those days, there were no public schools. Many people in Siberia did not know how to read. Parents who did know how to read taught their children at home, and when they were old enough, boys were sometimes sent to boarding school. These would be mostly priests' sons who wanted to go to seminary. The girls stayed at home until they married or became nuns.

In Orthodox homes, children were taught to read using the Psalter, the Bible, and church service books. This is how Eusebius taught John to read. John's mother and father believed that education was very important.

By the time he was seven, John was able to help with the reading in the church. This was something he loved to do. It made him happy to sing and pray in God's house.

1804.
John stands on a stool at the kliros, reading in the church at age seven. On the wall of the church, the icon on the right is of the Prophet Elias, since this is his Church.

8

For the Nativity (Christmas) services that year, the priest asked him to read the epistle. This was a big honor for a young boy. How his eyes must have shone!

ONE THING THAT MADE LIFE DIFFICULT was that John's father was sick for long periods. He had to lie in bed for days. He continued to teach John from his bedside.

When John was still young, his father died after making confession and receiving the Holy Gifts. How hard that must have been for little John, to lose his papa. The whole family was very sad. After the funeral, Eusebius Popov was buried in the village cemetery.

The father's death was especially hard on John's mother. She was pregnant with her fourth child and had no way of earning money. Women did not work outside the home in those days. How was she to feed four children? An uncle offered to take John into his home to help her out. That way she would only have three children to feed and clothe. Thekla Popov agreed to let John go.

John's uncle Dmitrii was a deacon in the church, as well as a watchmaker and mechanic. He was able to continue John's education and teach him about watches and machines. Later, when John became a father and a priest, he would use these skills to build his church and support his family. John paid close attention and worked hard. He was respectful and obedient. His uncle was pleased with him.

While John was at his uncle Dmitrii's house, his mother was thinking how to get him a better education. Since she had no money, she prayed to God for help. God answered her prayers, and soon someone sent John money for school.

When he was only nine and a half years old, John traveled to the city of Irkutsk to go to the seminary. This took a lot of courage, because he didn't know anyone in the seminary or the city. However, our all-good God, who sees all our troubles, sent Uncle Dmitrii to help John. Uncle Dmitrii's wife had died and he had become a hieromonk, a priest-monk. He was sent to Irkutsk, and so was able to help his little nephew.

Even with Uncle Dmitrii's kindness, life at the seminary was hard. In the winter, the temperature would sometimes drop to sixty degrees below zero (Fahrenheit)! The students' day started with Matins at four o'clock in the morning. John had to learn Latin and Greek. Also, the other boys teased him because of his country clothing. They

1818.
Seminarian John graduates from Irkutsk Seminary, which is affiliated with Ascension Monastery.

were city boys with fancier clothes and were sure they were better than he. But John didn't let that stop him. He worked hard and did his best.

More than anything, John loved to read. He read every history and science book in the school library. He also made things with his hands, because he was clever. From one of the books, he figured out how to make a water clock, all by himself. He made it out of scraps of wood. The face of the clock was a piece of paper. The ticking sound came from water dripping onto a pan from a birch root John had hollowed out. It took time and effort to figure out. At last it was finished, and it worked! When the other boys saw it, they admired it tremendously. John's next creation was a pocket sundial. (A sundial is an instrument that tells time using the sun.) Many boys asked him to make them one of their own. In this way, John made friends, and the boys stopped teasing him.

John grew to be six feet, three inches tall. He was one of the best students in the seminary. There were so many students named Popov, the head of the school could not keep them all straight. (Popov means "of the priests." It was as common as Smith would be today.) So he changed some of the students' names. That is how our John Popov became John Veniaminov. He was named after a holy bishop.

When he was nineteen years old, John asked permission to marry. In those days, when it was time to marry, the adults picked a wife for a young man. So a young woman named Katherine was found for John. They were soon married. Shortly after that, John was ordained a deacon. Deacon John began to teach religion classes for both boys and girls. This was unusual. In those days, most people didn't think girls needed education outside the home.

Seminary was so hard, most young men didn't graduate. Deacon John *did* graduate, and at the top of the class of 1818. This was because he was intelligent, worked hard, and didn't give up when things were difficult.

While in Irkutsk, Katherine and Father Deacon John had three daughters. All three died as babies. How sad the young parents must have been! Finally, God gave them a son, who lived. They named him Innocent, after Saint Innocent of Irkutsk.

2

A New Direction

I N 1821, DEACON JOHN was ordained a priest. He was assigned to one of the best parishes in the city. He and Katherine had a good life there and were happy. Father John might have stayed there all his life and been unknown to the world. But that was not God's plan.

In 1823, the Church decided to send a priest to the New World, to Unalaska, to serve the native people. (Unalaska is part of a chain of islands off the coast of Alaska. Alaska was owned by Russia at this time, so the Russian Orthodox Church needed to care for its people there.) They were having a hard time finding someone, however.

1821.
After John's ordination to the priesthood, he is assigned to the Irkutsk Annunciation Church, where he teaches with great zeal.

Everyone had heard that the weather was terrible and the land was filled with wild animals and savages. No one wanted to go.

Father John didn't want to go either. He served in a church where the people loved him, he owned his own home, and he and Katherine were happy. Besides, his salary was much bigger than the salary being offered. Why would he want to go anywhere, especially to Alaska?

Something happened that changed his mind, however. One of Father John's spiritual children had been to America. He thought it was wonderful, especially the Aleut people. He talked to Father John, trying to inspire him to go. Father John wasn't interested, no matter what the man said.

Right before this visitor was about to leave, he tried one last time. And this last time made all the difference. As Father John would say later, "When my friend began to tell me of the Aleuts' zeal in prayer and hearing the Word of God, suddenly, blessed be the name of the Lord! I began to burn with desire to go to such a people!" Now he could hardly wait to go. When Father John told Bishop Michael, the bishop agreed to send him. After all, there was no one else who would go.

Next, Father John had to tell his family. They were very unhappy about the idea and tried to change his mind. But Father John was firm. Out of love for God and Father John, they agreed as well. They left Irkutsk for America on May 7, 1823. Father John's wife Katherine, who was pregnant, their son Innocent, his mother Thekla, and his brother Stephen all went with Father John. They had to travel all the way across Siberia, 2,200 miles, to the port of Okhotsk. This is almost as far as from the west coast of the United

States to the east coast. (If there are maps of Russia in your home, you can look and see what a great journey this was.)

They traveled by horse-drawn cart, barge, and packhorse. The trip took three months and was very hard. Things were so bad, Father John said that it was like the plagues God sent to Pharaoh and the Egyptians. (You can

1823. *Father John and his family traveling across Siberia on horseback.*

read about the plagues in your Bible, in Exodus chapters 7–12.) After arriving in Okhotsk, they waited for a sailing ship. They set sail for America on August 30, 1823.

3

Arriving in Sitka

AFTER A TWO-MONTH OCEAN VOYAGE, Father John and his family arrived in Sitka, Alaska. The date was October 29, 1823. The United States of America had twenty-three states. The War of 1812 was over and the Erie Canal was being built. James Monroe was president. The Veniaminov family stayed in Sitka for the winter. A baby girl was born two weeks after they arrived. They named her Katherine, after her mother.

The following summer, the family sailed to Unalaska Island. At first, they lived in a house dug out of the earth, like the native Aleuts. The third day after their arrival was the Feast of the Procession of the Holy Cross. The first Divine Liturgy on the island was celebrated that day. Everyone was joyful.

Soon Father John built a house for his family and rebuilt the village church. The Aleut people loved to help him. Father John taught them carpentry, blacksmith work, and bricklaying. By working with the people, he learned their language and way of life. He waited until he understood them and the way they thought about things before teaching them. Then, when he *did* teach, he used examples they understood. The Aleut people had many beliefs that helped them understand the Christian faith. They had been prepared long before, by the Holy Spirit, to receive the Faith when it came.

Home and family were very important to Father John. He and Katherine had five more children in the years they lived on Unalaska. (That made seven children altogether, in addition to the three that died in Russia.) Father John was a loving father and a good husband. He used to say that the family is a home-church, like a small ship heading toward the Kingdom of heaven.

There was much work to do around the church and home. The whole family worked together. The children helped their father make candles, vestments, furniture, and musical instruments. They even helped him make the town clock! The youngest children held the hammer or handed their father tacks when needed. The older ones planed wood or glued parts together. The children loved to work with their father. This is how they learned the love of labor.

1824.
While living on Unalaska Island, Father John, with the help of Aleut workers, builds a church.

Being useful and working with their hands made them feel good.

Father John also taught his children to read and write, and gave lessons about nature and the law of God. They had a homemade weather station and kept weather records. When they weren't working or studying, he played ball with them, told stories, or took them on walks. They obeyed and respected their parents, who loved them so much.

Father John loved the native people he had come to serve. He and his wife started a school for both boys and girls. They taught crafts and trades, as well as reading and arithmetic. He also started a home for orphan girls and even a hospital. When people were sick, Father John visited and helped them.

THE VENIAMINOV FAMILY SPENT ten years on Unalaska. Father John made many trips to the Fox-Aleutian and Pribilof Islands, to visit the natives and serve them. He spent long days in a kayak, crossing hundreds of miles of ocean. (A kayak is a boat that is covered on top and made of animal skins. It is usually just big enough for one person.) His legs began to have terrible pains from sitting in a kayak for so many hours, in the cold, cold waters of the Bering Sea.

On land, he traveled by reindeer, dogsled, horse-drawn sleigh, bull, horseback, snowshoe, and on foot. His Russian clothing did not keep him warm enough. Soon he began to wear the clothes made by the natives, which were much better for that climate. The coat was made of forty to sixty woodpecker skins sewn together. To keep dry in the rain, he wore a shirt made out of the stomach of an animal, such as a bear, walrus, or whale. The shirt was called a *kamleika*. The natives rubbed these shirts with animal fat (which smelled horribly), so they would last longer. Father John also wore Aleutian boots made from seal flippers. What would his schoolmates have thought if they could see him now, in a woodpecker coat and seal-flipper boots?

During his travels, Father John's life was in danger many, many times. Once he was thirty miles offshore when water began to swamp his kayak. Father John dipped water out with a cup as fast as he could, and prayed to God. He later said, "I was continually in danger of losing my life, for, as they say, there's not a single board here to save you from death, just skins." But God always heard his prayers and saved His faithful servant.

When Father John and his helpers reached a village, they would stop for a few days. Father John taught the people about God, the Church, and living a Christian life. He wanted to make sure the people understood their faith. He was careful that the people became Christian for the right reasons, so he never gave presents to the newly baptized. Before, the people had been given gifts. They liked them so much, their friends and relatives would ask for baptism just in order to receive gifts. Some people would get baptized more than once just for the presents.

Father John didn't want that. He wanted the people to become true Christians. He wanted them to be inspired and love God in their hearts. For this, his best teaching tool was his own life. People could see how loving he was and how hard he worked for them. He was a real Christian, so they could see that being a Christian was a wonderful thing. They also saw, through his life, how they should live.

And what a life it was! On a typical day, Father John might serve Divine Liturgy, chrismate thirty-two people, marry eleven couples, and hear over a hundred confessions. He also served funerals and visited the sick. There might be a couple of hundred baptisms. He often worked late into the night, and he would still be up early the next morning.

1824—1834. *While in the Unalaska region, Father John visits various settlements, preaching and serving sacraments to all the natives.*

BECAUSE OF FATHER JOHN'S LOVE and respect for the people, they loved and respected him in return. Wherever he went, they left everything they were doing to listen to his sermons and teaching. Whole villages would come. One of the people wrote, "When he preached the Word of God, all the people listened, and they listened without moving until he stopped. Nobody thought of fishing or hunting. Nobody felt hungry or thirsty as long as he was speaking, not even little children."

Another person wrote, "This land is made glad by the arrival of Your Blessing to teach in these parts the Orthodox Christian faith." People even raised money to help the Veniaminov family with things they needed for their home.

The Aleuts believed in Jesus Christ with their whole mind and heart. They came to live a true Christian life, so that crime and even arguments were unknown among them. Before they became Christian, Aleuts had made totem poles. Now they used their artistic talents to make their churches beautiful. They made their own iconostases, icon frames, vestments, altar coverings, crosses, and other things needed for the church. The church became the center of village and family life, just as our Savior meant it to be.

Father John worked hard to learn the language of each of the peoples he worked with. One of the chiefs, John Pankov, helped him in this. John had been educated in Russia. He spoke Russian and Aleut perfectly. John taught Father John Aleut and interpreted for him when he preached.

As Father John worked to help form the native Church, there was one serious problem. The Aleut people had no written language. There were no books and there was no way to write things down. Father John decided that they needed to have a written language. This way, the Bible, church service books, and other books could be translated into Aleut. This would help them understand their Christian faith better. It would also allow them to hold church services in their own language.

1824—34. *Father John creates an Aleut grammar and alphabet and translates the Gospel into the Aleut language.*

Seeing this great need, Father John created an alphabet for the Aleut language. Once there was an alphabet, he wrote a book of grammar. Then he translated the Divine Liturgy, the Gospel of Saint Matthew, and a book of Christian teachings into Aleut. He even wrote schoolbooks in Aleut on different subjects.

The most famous book Father John wrote was for the Aleut people. It's called, *The Indication of the Way into the Kingdom of Heaven.* (You can still buy this book in Orthodox bookstores.) They sent the book to Russia to be printed. (There weren't any printing presses in Alaska.) The bishop in Russia thought the book was so wonderful that he had it translated into Russian and Slavonic. So it was published in three languages. The bishop rewarded Father John for his hard work. He gave him a pectoral cross and awarded him the Order of Saint Anne.

The first time the Aleuts heard the Gospel and Divine Liturgy in their own language, in 1831, was a great, historic day. When they saw books in their own language, they asked to have copies for themselves. With the help of these books, many Aleut people learned to read. The number of adults who could read was very high among the native people of Alaska, thanks to Father John. He is mentioned in Alaskan history books as one of the great educators of the people.

4

The Man Who Spoke with Angels

One of Father John's most amazing adventures happened on the island of Akim. When he arrived there for the first time, the whole village was standing on the shore, waiting for him. They were all dressed in their best clothes. Father John asked them why they were there. They answered, "We knew you left Unalaska for this island and would be here today. To show you our joy, we came to welcome you."

"How did you know I was coming?" Father John asked.

"Our shaman, the old man Smirennikov, told us," they said. (A shaman is a religious leader among the native peoples.) The shaman had said that a priest would come to teach them how to pray to God. He even described what Father John looked like.

Father John asked to meet their shaman. Father John asked John Smirennikov how he had known he was coming. John said that after his baptism, he began to be visited by two people he called "white men." No one else could see these white men but him. They were dressed like the angel Gabriel in the church icons. These men came almost every day and taught John about the Christian faith. With their help, John healed the sick, helped find food during times of famine, saw things that would happen in the future, and performed other miracles. The angels always said that what they told John was from God, not from themselves.

Father John and John Smirennikov talked a long time. John was unhappy that the people called him a shaman, because that was not what he was. Shamans believe in many gods, but he was a Christian. Christians believe in the one, true God. Father John decided that the men who visited John were real angels, sent by God.

1828. *When visiting Akim Island, Father John talks with John Smirennikov, who speaks with angels almost every day.*

Father John asked if the angels would talk with *him*. John asked the angels, who said that they would. The two men walked together toward the place where the angels were to meet them. On the way, Father John was thinking about the idea of talking to real angels. He knew that only the saints talk to angels, because the saints are pure in heart. Father John didn't believe he was a saint or pure in heart. He began to think he should not go; he wasn't worthy. So he turned back. Instead, he wrote a report about John and the angels. This was sent to his bishop.

The bishop wrote back, praising Father John for being humble but asking him to meet with the angels for the sake of the Church. However, by the time the report reached Russia and the bishop's answer came back to Unalaska, three years had passed. By that time, John Smirennikov had died. So Father John never talked to the angels.

One Russian man wrote about John Smirennikov, saying that the angels' visits show God's great love for all people. He sent His angels to teach John, so the people would believe in the Gospel when it was preached to them.

The Orthodox Church celebrates John Smirennikov as someone who is blessed. We believe he is in heaven and prays for us, because he pleased God while he lived on earth.

Blessed John Smirennikov, pray to God for us!

5

From Sitka to California

ALASKA WAS NOT AN EASY PLACE to live. In the harsh climate, Father John's health became worse every year. He asked his bishop to send him to Sitka. The bishop agreed. As Father John and his family boarded the ship for Sitka, the villagers came to say goodbye. They all cried as he set sail, they loved him so much.

The natives around Sitka call themselves Tlingit. The Russians called them Kolosh, from the word for "peg," because of the lip-plugs worn by the women. The local Russians said that the Kolosh were fierce and bloodthirsty.

1834—38.
In Sitka, Father John befriends the Tlingit natives. Sitka's patron saint, the Archangel Michael, is shown in the background. (Sitka was first named "New Archangel.")

Father John wanted to go see these people, but he couldn't go right away. This turned out to be God's blessing. The Tlingits soon became sick from smallpox. But they would not take the Russian medicine. So the Russians lived, while hundreds of natives died. If Father John had gone earlier, they would have believed he had brought the smallpox and they never would have accepted him. As it was, the smallpox was over by the time he came.

As he had with the Aleuts, Father John studied the Tlingit language and made an alphabet for them. The first time he celebrated Divine Liturgy there, 1,500 people came! They were quiet and respectful through the whole service. Even the children made no noise and stood still. After the services, they asked questions and Father John taught them. The people came to love him, and most of them were baptized. They were not bad, as the Russians had said, when treated with respect and love.

WHILE IN SITKA, Father John had the chance to sail down the coast to California. There was a church at Fort Ross that needed a priest. Father John landed at Bodega Bay and rode horseback north to the fort. There he held church services. He also baptized and married people.

Nearby, there lived some Catholic priests. Father John went to visit them. They had a pleasant time together, speaking in Latin! It was the only language they all knew. The priests learned that Father John made barrel organs. They didn't have an organ, so they asked him to make them one. When Father John sent the organ, he sent along sheets of church music and Russian dance songs. When he heard how much they liked the music, Father John was pleased. He later said, "Those priests are probably still praying to God to the music of our merry Russian dances!"

You can visit Fort Ross today. It is on the coast of northern California. The old fort burned down, but they built another in its place that looks very much like the original. One exhibit in the museum has a note about Father John Veniaminov's visit in 1836. In 1997, to celebrate the two-hundredth anniversary of Saint Innocent's birth, a Vigil was served in the fort chapel.

6

Returning to Russia

I N 1838, AFTER FOUR YEARS IN SITKA, the Veniaminovs were ready to return to Russia. Katherine and four of the children sailed west to Okhotsk. From there, they would journey over land to Irkutsk.

Father John and his daughter Thekla traveled east, because they were going to Saint Petersburg. This meant taking a sailing ship halfway around the world! (If you have a globe at your home, you can see where they went.) They first sailed south, through the North Pacific and South Pacific, around Cape Horn, then north through the Atlantic Ocean, the North Sea, and the Baltic Sea, to the port of Kronstadt. On the way, they stopped at Hawaii, Tahiti, Rio de Janeiro, England, and Denmark. They spent four days in Tahiti. There they saw monkeys, palm trees, pineapple trees, tropical birds, brilliant flowers, and other marvelous things. What a difference from Siberia and Alaska, to be in a tropical paradise where it never snowed!

Their trip took eight months. Father John brought Thekla to a girls' school in Saint Petersburg. There he presented reports to the Holy Synod. In the reports, Father John asked the Synod for more churches and priests to serve the people in America.

Next Father John traveled to Moscow, where he was presented to Metropolitan Philaret. The Metropolitan liked him very much. He saw that Father John was humble, simple, and truthful. Metropolitan Philaret believed these qualities were important in a man. Whenever someone spoke of Father John, the Metropolitan would say, "There is something apostolic about that man. My wish is that he would become metropolitan after me." ("Apostolic" means that Father John was like the twelve Apostles of Jesus Christ.

1838. *Fr. John visits Russia and meets Metropolitan Philaret.*

That's a very great thing to say about someone.) On the Feast of the Nativity, 1839, Metropolitan Philaret honored Father John by making him an archpriest.

While he was in Russia, *everyone* wanted to meet Father John. He was famous both as a missionary and as a scientist. He had written many scientific reports about Alaska, which were read at the Academy of Sciences. His missionary trips had been reported in the Russian newspapers. The foreign newspapers called him "the Apostle of the North." The most noble families in Russia received him and gave donations for his work. People gave him not only money, but also vestments, icons, and other things for the American churches.

Father John was also presented to Tsar Nicholas I. The tsar thought highly of him. He invited Father John to the royal apartments to meet the tsarina, tsarevich, and royal princesses. They all came to love Father John. He spent many hours with them, telling the tsarevich and young princesses all about his wonderful adventures in the New World.

WHILE HE WAS IN MOSCOW, some sad news came to Father John. His wife had died on November 25. (She died on the feast day of her name saint, Saint Katherine of Alexandria. This shows that she was close to her patron saint.)

This was very hard on Father John, who missed her very much. One of the people who tried to comfort him was Metropolitan Philaret. He suggested that Father John become a monk, which was what widowed priests usually did. Father John needed to think and pray about this. He made a pilgrimage to the Holy Trinity-Saint Sergius Lavra.

There he offered pannikhidas for his wife and prayed, asking God what he should do. He stayed three days, but came to no decision.

While he was away, the Holy Synod met. They read and accepted Father John's reports on the American mission. They agreed with his idea to create more churches and send more priests. They were very impressed with his work—so much so that they asked Father John to write a book that would be used to train new missionaries.

Father John was glad to write the book. He gave it careful thought and spent a lot of time writing it. The opening words were, "To bring the light of the Gospel to those who have not yet seen this saving light, is truly a holy work, like that of the Apostles. Blessed is he who with zeal and

1839.
Father John makes a second pilgrimage to pray about becoming a monk, this time to the Kiev Caves Monastery.

love works to convert such people. Great will be his reward in heaven." The book was used for many years throughout the Russian Empire.

One year passed. Father John still couldn't decide whether he should become a monk. He wondered what would happen to his children. He also thought it would be hard to keep the prayer rule of a monk on his long missionary journeys. He went to the Kiev Caves Monastery to pray and think some more.

While he was away, Metropolitan Philaret and Tsar Nicholas made a plan. They decided to place all the Veniaminov children in excellent schools. They also found the children kind people who would watch out for them and act in the place of a parent. This way the children would be well taken care of and Father John would be free to become a monk.

When Father John returned to Saint Petersburg, they told him their plan. Father John was pleased. The way seemed clear to him now, and he agreed to become a monk.

7

Becoming a Monk, then a Bishop

IN ORDER TO BECOME A MONK, Father John had to write a formal letter to the Holy Synod. In it, he wrote that after the tonsure, he wanted to continue his missionary work. (This would be an exception to the usual rule of monks living in a monastery.) The Synod agreed.

The tonsure took place at the Holy Trinity-Saint Sergius Lavra. It was performed by Metropolitan Philaret and Bishop Ignatius Brianchaninov. (The Church now glorifies both of these men as saints.) He was given a new name, Father Innocent, after Saint Innocent of Irkutsk. During

1840. *Father John is tonsured as a monk by Saints Philaret and Ignatius Brianchaninov. Saint Innocent of Irkutsk, Father Innocent's new patron saint, is shown in the icon above.*

Divine Liturgy the next day, Father Innocent was made an archimandrite. Archimandrite Innocent had entered the angelic life. (This is how the Church sees the life of a monk or nun. It is like the life of the angels: a hymn of praise to God.)

WHILE HE WAS IN RUSSIA, a big decision was made about Alaska that changed Father Innocent's life. One of the greatest needs of the people in Alaska was to have their own bishop. Their own bishop would know their needs and care for them better than one in Russia. This was one of the most important requests in Father John's reports. The Holy Synod and the tsar thought this over and agreed. They made a new diocese of Alaska and added to it the eastern seaboard of Siberia, Kamchatka, and the Kurile Islands. The next question was, who should be the bishop of the new diocese?

The third day after his tonsure, Archimandrite Innocent was brought before Tsar Nicholas I. Father Innocent gave the tsar a gift of an icon of Jesus Christ. The two men talked. The tsar asked Father Innocent about his work. Finally, the tsar said the new diocese of Alaska and Kamchatka was approved. "But," he asked, "who should be its bishop?"

"The Holy Spirit will inspire in Your Majesty's heart the holy idea of whom to pick," Father Innocent answered.

The tsar was quiet for a minute. Then he said, "I wish to make *you* bishop of Kamchatka."

Father Innocent was stunned. He hadn't expected this! "I am wholly at Your Majesty's command. Whatever pleases you is holy in my sight."

1840. *Archimandrite Innocent visits with Emperor Nicholas.*

"Very well. Tell the Metropolitan."

And so it was decided. Father Innocent was to become a bishop.

Earlier, the tsar himself had added the Kurile Islands to the new diocese. Someone objected that there were no churches there. The tsar had answered, "He will build

1840. *Archimandrite Innocent is consecrated as a bishop. The Kazan icon of the Mother of God is shown above, as this took place in her cathedral.*

some!" Such was the tsar's faith in our holy father.

Before his consecration, Archimandrite Innocent gave a speech to the Holy Synod: "What wonderful mercy God has shown to me. Blessed be the Lord who perfects His power in weakness and who chooses the humble and unworthy. The more these things are unexpected, the more clearly I see in them the finger of God. Lord, all my hope is before You and from You: do Your will in me and through me. Grant me new desire and new strength to be of use to my Church and my nation. Pray to the Lord that His grace and mercy may be with me forever."

THE CONSECRATION OF A BISHOP doesn't happen very often. It is a holy and great occasion. On December 15, 1840, the Cathedral of the Kazan Icon of the Theotokos was filled with people. Four bishops served and consecrated the new bishop. After this, Bishop Innocent was ready to return to America.

Before he left, Metropolitan Philaret gave Bishop Innocent many gifts, including an ancient icon from the Holy Trinity-Saint Sergius Lavra. He also let Bishop Innocent take with him any of the monks he wished. The gifts Bishop Innocent received for his mission filled two sleds.

Before returning to America, Bishop Innocent wanted to visit his children. After all, he wouldn't see them again for years. So the new bishop traveled 2,600 miles overland to Irkutsk. Along the way, he talked to other bishops, to get their advice about his new work.

When he arrived in Irkutsk, the bells of every church in the city rang and rang. They were welcoming home their first son to become a bishop. Crowds of people came out to see him. It was a holiday for the whole city. That Sunday, Bishop Innocent served Divine Liturgy in the church where he had been ordained a priest. His old schoolmates, some of whom had teased him for his country clothes, came to receive his blessing.

Bishop Innocent stayed in Irkutsk one month, visiting his children and old friends. One of his teachers from seminary came to visit and knelt at his feet. Bishop Innocent helped him up, saying, "You ought not to kneel before me, but I before you. Through you I went out into the world." Then the bishop knelt before his old teacher.

Bishop Innocent also visited the relics of his new patron

saint, Saint Innocent of Irkutsk. The city spent the month collecting vestments, linens, necessary items, and money for the American mission.

All too soon, Bishop Innocent was on his way again. The bishop made one stop in Anga. There he visited the house where he was born and the graves of his parents and wife. Six weeks later, the bishop and his staff reached Okhotsk. On August 20, they set sail for America.

It takes many days to sail from Siberia to Alaska. Towards the end of their journey, Bishop Innocent held a Vigil for Saint John the Evangelist on the deck of the ship. The northern lights overhead were as beautiful as any cathedral a bishop could ask for.

8

Bishop Innocent, Serving in Alaska

BISHOP INNOCENT ARRIVED AT SITKA on September 25, 1840. At that time, Martin Van Buren was president of the United States and the Missouri Compromise was in effect. The United States was having trouble with Mexico. They would be at war by 1846. The American people on the east coast of North America and the Russian people on the west coast still had no direct contact with each other.

In Sitka, the new bishop eagerly set to work. As a bishop, he was able to serve the people in new ways. He started new schools and sent missionary priests to where they were needed. Somehow, he also found the time to make a clock for the cathedral. He was even busier than ever.

One thing made life in Sitka especially pleasant for Bishop Innocent. His daughter Katherine and her family were now living there. Katherine's husband was a priest. Bishop Innocent sent him to a new mission on the Alaskan mainland.

While in Sitka, Bishop Innocent had another amazing adventure. He went for a walk one day and found a wounded eagle. When he walked over to it, the eagle let itself be picked up. The bishop took the bird home and lovingly nursed it. When the wing healed, Bishop Innocent took the eagle up to a hill so it could fly back to the wild. But the bird wouldn't fly away. Not knowing what else to do, the bishop brought it back home. The second time he took the bird out, it flew away.

Some time later, Bishop Innocent was standing outside his house. The eagle he had taken care of flew down to him and stood before him. It bowed down to him three times, just as you are supposed to do to a bishop! Then it flew away again.

1841. *Bishop Innocent nurses a wounded eagle. Saint Herman and Spruce Island, complete with Saint Herman's little chapel, can be seen on the right.*

(In the lives of the saints, there are many other examples of wild animals that were not afraid of the saints. Some animals became their friends and servants. Saint Gerasim had a lion that carried water pots on his back for him. Saint Seraphim of Sarov had a bear that came to him every day for a meal. These things happen to the saints because they are so close to God. They become as Adam was in Paradise.)

ANOTHER OF SAINT INNOCENT'S ADVENTURES concerned another saint, Saint Herman of Alaska. Perhaps you know about him already. But if you don't, he is a wonderful saint to learn about. Saint Herman came from Russia to Alaska with other monks in 1794. After a while, he came to live on Spruce Island by himself. There he took care of orphan children and served the native people. Someone once asked Saint Herman if he was lonely. He said, "No! I am not alone! God is here, as He is everywhere. Holy angels are here. With whom is it better to talk, with men or with angels? Of course, with angels!"

The night Father Herman died, people from another island saw a pillar of light that went from Spruce Island to heaven. That was five years before the event we are about to describe. Father Herman and Bishop Innocent lived during the same time. The two men never met, but Bishop Innocent heard of Father Herman and his work.

Bishop Innocent had set sail on a trip that was supposed to be short. However, a fierce headwind came up that prevented the ship from sailing where they needed to go. Fifty-two souls were crowded below deck as tall waves crashed over the ship. Instead of three days, their journey had lasted twenty-eight days so far. Water and food were running out. Shipwreck or starvation seemed certain.

Then the captain noticed they were near Spruce Island. When Bishop Innocent learned this, he prayed, "Father Herman, if you have found favor with God, let the winds change." Less than fifteen minutes later, the wind changed. They sailed into harbor at Spruce Island with no further trouble. There Bishop Innocent served a moleben of thanksgiving to Father Herman on his grave. (The Church glorified Father Herman as a saint in 1970.)

1841. *Bishop Innocent is saved by the prayers of St. Herman.*

AFTER THIS TRIP, BISHOP INNOCENT spent the winter in Sitka. While waiting through the Alaskan winter, Bishop Innocent decided he needed to visit his whole diocese. He wanted to meet the people himself, so he would know them and their needs. But you can hardly imagine what a trip that would be!

There has never been such a large diocese in the history of the Church. If you look on the map, you will hardly believe it. It started in Okhotsk and stretched all the way across the Pacific Ocean to Sitka. Then it went south to Fort Ross, California. It was about 3,600 miles across and 1,800 miles long.

Remember, there were no cars or airplanes in those days. It would take a year and four months to make that kind of trip. But Bishop Innocent was not afraid of such a long, difficult journey.

After Pascha, Bishop Innocent set off. He traveled 12,400 miles in sixteen months, by ship, kayak, reindeer, bull, horseback, dogsled, and snowshoe. His work this time was different from his travels as a priest. As bishop, he was in charge of the Church and its priests. Wherever he went, he wanted to make sure everything was done properly and the people were well cared for. Everywhere he went, he served the sacraments, preached, taught the people, inspected everything, and looked at church records.

Bishop Innocent's first stop was Unalaska. This was a special visit, because he had lived there for ten years. He arranged it so the ship arrived on the Feast of the Ascension. This was the feast of the local church, so it was a big day for the people there. As the bishop arrived, all the bells rang and the people ran from everywhere to greet him with great joy. He served Divine Liturgy in the church he had built with his own hands sixteen years before.

Bishop Innocent spent more than a month there, visiting with almost every Aleut. Since he had been gone, the people had continued and grown in their Christian faith. Most of them were reading the books he had published for them. They had tremendous love and respect for their spiritual father. When the time came for him to leave, the Aleuts presented him with an eagle rug they had made from native roots and grasses. (An eagle rug is a special rug a bishop stands on in church.) It was a visit they would all remember for years to come.

Soon after visiting Unalaska, they stopped at the island of Atka. There Bishop Innocent met the missionary priest, Father Yakov (James) Netsvetov. Father Yakov was an Alaskan native, born on Saint George Island in 1804. When he was old enough, Yakov was sent to the seminary in Irkutsk for his education. (This was the same school Bishop Innocent had attended.) After Yakov became a priest, he and his wife were sent to the island of Atka.

When he arrived, the village of Atka had seven houses. Father Yakov began holding church in a tent, but soon built a church. All the Aleuts were already baptized, so he gave classes to teach about the Faith. He also traveled to other Aleutian islands and performed weddings and baptisms, held services, and taught the people. Father Yakov used a *baidarka* (a local kind of kayak) to go from island to island.

In 1833, Father Yakov's home burned down and his wife died. It was a hard year for him. But he didn't stop

1842.
Bishop Innocent meets Saint Yakov Netsvetov.

working. He began to translate the Bible into the native language. Bishop Innocent liked Father Yakov and saw how valuable he was as a missionary. He sent him to the Yukon, far north in Alaska. Father Yakov served the people there until two years before his death. He died on July 26, 1864. The Church has glorified Father Yakov as a saint. He is our first native apostolic saint in America.

LIKE FATHER YAKOV, Bishop Innocent's priests and staff loved him. One priest wrote, "He was not so much a boss as a father who loved his children. He took an active interest in his priests' problems." Bishop Innocent would sometimes give them extra money, because their pay was so low. One of the priests wrote about his meeting with the bishop. This was soon after the priest's wedding.

The bishop greeted him, "Well, Father Athanasius, I hear you used up all your money on your wedding."

"Yes, Your Eminence."

"Okay. I'd like to give you some extra money. But only under certain conditions. Will you meet them?"

"Why not, if they are easy?"

"Don't worry. My conditions are very light. First, your hair doesn't look right. Buy yourself a comb and some hair tonic."

"I have a comb—here it is. But I don't like hair tonic."

"Okay, then I'll tell you what to do. When you take a bath, wash your hair and put butter on it. Then lie down somewhere where it's warm. The butter will soak in and your hair will be soft as silk."

"I'll do it."

"Good. Next, you need glasses. You're going to ruin your eyes."

"I tried glasses. They hurt my eyes. So I stopped. It's true that I can't see far away. But this way there's less temptation."

"But you'll be sorry when you're old. Take care of your eyes now and you'll be glad when you are older."

"All right, Your Eminence. I'll give glasses another try."

"Good. Now here's the third condition. When you serve Divine Liturgy, your phelonion is always slipping to one side. That doesn't look very nice."

"What can I do, Your Eminence? I don't have one that fits me."

"Okay, tell my staff I said to sew you one that fits."

"Yes, Your Eminence!"

Another time, Bishop Innocent was talking with one of his deacons. The deacon asked, "Your Grace, if God is Love and all Mercy, why does He shut some people out of the Kingdom of heaven?"

"And why do you keep twisting your head about from side to side?" Bishop Innocent asked him. "Why don't you sit still?"

"Because the sun keeps hitting me right in the eye and just won't leave me in peace," the deacon replied.

"There. You've just answered your own question," the bishop laughed. "God does not shut out sinners who don't repent from His heavenly Kingdom. But they simply can't bear its light—any more than you can bear the light of the sun."

Bishop Innocent was easy to talk to, cheerful, and loved a good joke. He gave nicknames to some people. One priest who hardly ever talked he called "Gabby." A doctor who talked too much he called "Mum." When there were quarrels, he wanted people to work things out together, as though they were one family. (Before, when there were problems, the priests had complained to the bishop. That usually made things worse.) The priests and people loved their bishop deeply.

9

Long and Dangerous Journeys

As HE TRAVELED, Bishop Innocent spent a great deal of time on sailing ships. He would carefully watch the crew as they worked. He learned so much about sailing, one seaman said the bishop could command a ship by himself.

In fact, he saved one ship from sinking. They had sailed in a deep fog all night. The bishop suddenly woke up and asked the captain, "What's our speed and heading?" The captain told him. The bishop continued, "Can you see the rocks near the Kurile Islands yet? We should be near them. The current is strong here."

The bishop hurried up on deck and looked around. Then he told the captain to change course. The captain obeyed him. The ship had just changed direction when the fog lifted. There were the rocks! If they hadn't changed course, the ship would have broken into pieces on the rocks. They would all have been drowned!

When they arrived at Fox Island, most of the natives were sick. Bishop Innocent stayed a while to help them. Through the bishop's prayers, many miracles of healing occurred.

Bishop Innocent had a great respect for the native people. He wrote that many native Christian people were morally better than many Russians. He was especially impressed with how much the native people loved God. He

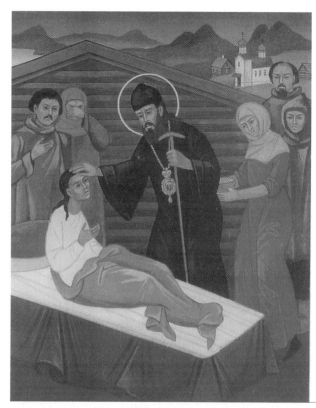

1842.
While on Fox Island, Bishop Innocent heals a sick woman.

liked to tell about one Tungus man who amazed the bishop with his faith. The man said, "Tungus always pray. Tungus know God give all. If I just kill one bird for food, I know it's God who give all things. If I don't make kill, I know it's because God not give me anything. This mean I bad and so I pray to God."

AT LAST, BISHOP INNOCENT ARRIVED at the port of Petropavlovsk, on Kamchatka. On the dock, the whole city was waiting for him. There were the governor in his best suit, the clergy in splendid vestments, the military in full dress uniforms, men in frock coats, and ladies in silk. Many of them had never seen a bishop before. It was a holiday for the whole city; all work stopped. Governor Nicholas Strannoliubskii and Father Gromov gave speeches. Afterward, everyone went to the cathedral to pray. Bishop Innocent spent several days in Petropavlovsk, looking into things to see how he could help.

One of the problems in the city was that the children were getting into a lot of trouble. This was because they didn't have enough to do. Bishop Innocent started classes for them. When he came back to the city months later, they were happier and better behaved. They also understood their Christian faith better. He saw that they would bow and make the sign of the cross as they went by a church. This shows understanding and respect for the House of God.

After a few days, the bishop left the city and traveled inland. He traveled more than 3,300 miles by reindeer or dogsled. Reindeer were hard to ride. But dogsleds weren't easy either. There were six dogs to a sled. It was so cold they had to carry the water bottles under their shirts to keep the water from freezing.

Sometimes the dogs would smell something and run away in the wrong direction. The sled would turn over and be dragged on its side. The driver would yell, "Ko! Ko! Ko!" This was to make the dogs stop. Finally the dogs would stop and they could put the sled upright.

There were also many dangers on these trips. There were packs of wolves in the forests. Blizzards could come up without warning. This was *very* dangerous. A blizzard could completely bury a dogsled, because it would snow so hard, so fast.

There were other kinds of dangers, too. One time, when

the bishop was traveling from Gizhiga to Tauisk, the road became a narrow cliff of ice, twelve feet above the sea. This part of the road was a mile long. If the temperature rose above freezing, there would be no road. Even if it stayed cold, the sleds could easily slide off into the sea. Bishop Innocent prayed hard, and all their sleds crossed safely.

Another time, in order to reach the village of Drain, they had to climb down a deep, deep ravine. The people tied ropes around Bishop Innocent and lowered him down the cliff. He had to find footholds in the snow as he went down. One priest took an animal hide and slid down the cliff, as if on a sled. The dogs and sleds were lowered down by ropes.

When they were all down, they went by dogsled sixty miles up the ravine, to a second cliff. This cliff was sheer ice. It was like glass and went almost straight down. Each person had to go hand-over-hand, alone, along the cliff. If they slipped, they would fall to a certain death in the darkness below. One by one, slowly, slowly, the party went down the cliff. They were very thankful when they all reached the bottom safely! At last, they arrived at Drain. Thus, Bishop Innocent was able to serve a people who were almost completely cut off from the rest of the world.

As Bishop Innocent traveled around Kamchatka, he saw an important need. He wrote, "There is no place where a person can go to be free of the noise of the world and save his soul." So he started a monastery. Monasteries are a blessing to the entire region and people where they are located. So this was a great thing.

After many months of travel covering over 12,000 miles by land and sea, the bishop returned to Sitka.

A COUPLE OF YEARS LATER, in 1846, Bishop Innocent made another tour of eastern Siberia. While he was in Ayan, the natives came to talk with him. "We wanted to visit you and see your yurts," they told him.

Bishop Innocent asked them, "I hear some people are making trouble. They try to scare you by saying that a priest will come and hurt you. Is this true?"

"Yes."

"Whoever said that is a bad person. I'm the chief of the priests here. No one will hurt you. If one of them does, you just tell Dmitrii Ivanovich and I'll get rid of him."

The people were happy to hear this. In another town, the priest was demanding furs in payment for weddings and refusing to serve Communion. Bishop Innocent looked into the matter. Finding out that things were not right, he removed the priest from his position. Another priest was put in his place.

In every church he visited, Bishop Innocent asked if the people were pleased with their priest. Most of the time, the answer was, "Yes!" One of the priests who received the most praise from his people was Father Stephen Veniaminov, the bishop's brother. They were joyful to see one another. Father Stephen decided to travel with his brother and help him find his way in the wilderness.

On this trip, the bishop traveled 14,850 miles in fourteen months.

10

A Man of Learning

BACK IN SITKA, BISHOP INNOCENT began work on something he'd thought about for a long time. The people needed a seminary and lower school. As things were, they had to travel to Russia in order to be trained as priests. This took a long time and was difficult. There weren't many American priests because of this. In order for the Church in America to grow, it needed American clergy. And for that to happen, it needed an American seminary.

Work on the new school began right away. Bishop Innocent wanted his priests to learn math, history, medicine, geography, penmanship, science, ship sailing, gardening, and the Bible. The seminary was a great blessing to the Orthodox people in America. Now, many more native men could become priests and serve their own people.

Bishop Innocent was a great believer in education, which is why he started so many schools and wrote so many books. He himself read and studied all his life. He knew a lot about mathematics, astronomy, physics, chemistry, natural science, and many other subjects. He was so well known for knowing about almost everything that people tried to find things he *didn't* know about.

Once a sailor showed him a photograph, thinking the bishop would not have seen one. A photograph was a rare thing in that region in those days. Not many people even knew photographs existed. Bishop Innocent, however, took it and explained the process by which it was made. He gave the names of the best photographers in Europe. Then he told the history of photography. The sailor was amazed.

Another time, a naval officer had a watch that had stopped working. He didn't think anyone but the bishop could fix it. But he felt funny about asking Bishop Innocent to fix his watch. So he invited the bishop over to dinner and left the watch out. Sure enough, the bishop saw the watch and asked about it. The officer complained that it didn't work. The bishop spent a minute or two with the watch, and then held it up. It was ticking. The bishop laughed and said, "You must know, a watch won't work unless you wind it!"

Bishop Innocent spent years keeping records of temperatures, cloud formations, rainfall, tides, currents, wind speed, and other such things. These were made into reports and sent to the Academy of Sciences. These reports were valuable to other scientists.

Bishop Innocent's scientific work also helped in practical ways. He is credited with saving the Pacific seals from becoming extinct. The Russian American Company was killing seals in large numbers. If this continued, the seals would all die out. Bishop Innocent noticed this. He studied the problem and made suggestions to the company of ways they should change the seal harvest. His suggestions were accepted and used. The seal herd was saved, thanks to the efforts of this great Orthodox ecologist.

The famous geographer, Admiral Theodore Luke (1797–1882), also made use of Bishop Innocent's observations. Admiral Luke and Bishop Innocent had become

1844.
*Bishop Innocent
meets the famous
geographer
Admiral Luke.*

friends when the bishop was living on Unalaska. The Admiral was a God-loving man who had received many awards as a sailor and scientist. He helped get Bishop Innocent's scientific reports published in Russia.

During this time, the bishop's son Gabriel arrived in Sitka. This made the bishop very happy. Gabriel had finished school in Russia and had come to help his father. Bishop Innocent tonsured him a reader and put him to work. Gabriel stayed in Sitka for three years. Then he went back to Moscow to find a bride, so he could be ordained a priest. (In the Orthodox Church, a man must either be a monk or married, before he can be ordained a priest.) Gabriel wanted to be a missionary priest, like his father.

Later, Father Gabriel and his wife Katherine were assigned to Kamchatka as missionaries.

In 1850, Bishop Innocent traveled again to Siberia to inspect that part of his diocese. In Petropavlovsk, he received an important message. He had been made an archbishop because of his loving service to the people and the Church.

11

His Diocese Expands

DURING THIS 1850 TRIP TO RUSSIA, Bishop Innocent visited Yakutsk. (This city is about 500 miles inland on the Lena River.) The people in this area didn't have houses to live in. They followed their animals from place to place. When they stopped, they set up yurts that they carried with them. They lived very much like the Plains Indians in America.

Because of this, a church might have 14,500 members, but none of the people lived near enough to attend church. The average number of people at Divine Liturgy was ten. Some Yakuts had never even seen a priest. Bishop Innocent wanted to help these people and wanted Yakutsk added to his diocese. That way he could get more priests and churches into the area.

The Synod accepted Bishop Innocent's offer. Yakutsk now became the center of the bishop's work. When he heard of the Synod's decision, Bishop Innocent set out to see the people in this new part of his diocese. He traveled along the Lena River, going 2,640 miles in six weeks. The Yakuts loved Bishop Innocent. They cleared a 200-mile-long road just for him. The people came from far away to wait at places where he would change horses, just to receive his blessing. After receiving it, they would return home.

The Yakuts had two important needs: more priests, and church service books written in their own language. Bishop

Innocent set to work at once. He got a group of people together to translate the Gospel and church service books into Yakut. A Russian writer named Ivan Goncharov was living in Yakutsk at the time. He helped in this work, which was hard. There are many words in Russian that the Yakuts don't know about. For example, there is no fruit in the

1853. *Bishop Innocent travels in a sleigh with Ivan Goncharov through Yakutsk, which has become the center of the Bishop's missionary labors.*

whole Yakutia region except berries. So there's no Yakut word for fruit. (How can you talk about Christians "bearing fruit" without the word "fruit"?) The translators decided to use Russian words sometimes, because they didn't know what else to do.

After a great deal of work, at last they were ready to celebrate the Divine Liturgy in the Yakut language. On July 19, 1859, the Cathedral of the Holy Trinity was filled with people. People had come from far away for the celebration. They were overjoyed to hear the divine service in their own language. Many knelt, others cried. After the service, the chiefs of the tribes came to Bishop Innocent. They asked him to make this day a yearly feastday for the people. To this day, July 19 is a great feastday for the people of the Yakutia region.

FROM 1853 TO 1856, THE CRIMEAN WAR was being fought. Russia fought England, France, and Sardinia. During this time, Archbishop Innocent's travels took him to Ayan. This town was in the area where the war was going on. As the archbishop and his people came near, they met Russians who were running away. They were terrified, saying the British were killing people and destroying everything.

Archbishop Innocent decided that he was needed in Ayan, because of the war. Showing great courage, he and two of his men entered the town. He went straight to the church. It had been searched by the British, but nothing had been stolen. As the battle ended, people began to come out of hiding. The archbishop helped them and they all prayed together.

Then several British warships sailed into the harbor.

Most of the Russians left town, fearing they would be killed. Archbishop Innocent stayed behind. That night, he and some of the Russians were in church, praying. The British second-in-command came ashore. He and his men came to the church to arrest the archbishop. This was not because he had done anything wrong, but because their two countries were at war.

The British came into the church, making a lot of noise. (Of course, you're supposed to be very quiet in church.) They saw the archbishop on his knees in the altar, praying. Archbishop Innocent paid no attention to them. He continued to pray out loud, in a clear, unhurried voice. The British were impressed with his peaceful manner and the holy expression on his face. They quieted down and waited. (Bishop Innocent said later that if they had known what he was praying for, they would have stopped him.)

When the church service was over, the soldiers said that they had come to arrest him. (They spoke through an interpreter, a person who spoke both Russian and English.) Archbishop Innocent said, "You have no need of me. I'm not a soldier. You'll just have to feed me." He invited them to his house for tea. They came and had a pleasant chat. Archbishop Innocent persuaded them to let him stay free for the time being. He even got them to free another priest who had been arrested.

The next day, the British returned, telling the archbishop that he could remain free. Also, their commander, Lord Charles Elliot, wanted to meet him onboard his warship. Lord Elliot received the archbishop with great honor. In the next few weeks, they spent many pleasant evenings together. Before he left, Lord Elliot had come to have great respect for this daring, courageous Russian bishop. He even had a picture made of Bishop Innocent to take home with him to England.

The Crimean War ended in 1856. In 1858, the Amur and Ussurijsk provinces were given to Russia peacefully. On May 18, Archbishop Innocent served a moleben on the banks of the Amur River, thanking God for His mercy.

ARCHBISHOP INNOCENT LOST NO TIME in bringing the church sacraments to the Amur and Ussurijsk provinces. He built a church on the Amur River and named it Blagoveshchensk

1858. *Archbishop Innocent holds a service on the shore of the Amur River. The Amur forms the natural boundary between Russia and China. Chinese Orthodox are shown on the other shore.*

(the Annunciation). The town was also renamed Blago-veshchensk.

By now the archbishop's diocese went from Yakutsk and Blagoveschensk in the west, to Sitka and Fort Ross in the east. It was the largest diocese in the two-thousand-year history of the Orthodox Church. Archbishop Innocent wrote to the Synod many times, asking for more bishops to help care for such a large area. The Synod found a bishop for Sitka, and promised one for Yakutsk.

This help was much needed. The years of travel and work were having their effect on the holy and aging archbishop. He became seriously ill and was in bed for a while. After he felt better, Archbishop Innocent wrote, "It seems

1858.
Archbishop Innocent renames the town of Blagoveshchensk and builds New Valaam Monastery there.

to me that I'll not live much longer." He was in pain most of the time. He also began to go blind from a disease of the eyes called cataracts.

None of these problems stopped him from continuing his missionary travels and work for the diocese. Archbishop Innocent always said, "No matter how difficult the travel, or how little the money, a bishop must visit every part of his diocese."

He found that the Amur region had rich soil and good harvests. Unfortunately, the Russians in the area were not God-loving. They did not care about their souls and were difficult to work with. But the archbishop did not become discouraged. He lived in Blagoveschensk for two months, ministering to the native people and setting things in order. He also built a monastery there, named New Valaam Monastery. The monastery would be a blessing to the Russian and native peoples in the area. It would also be the home of the new bishop, when he came.

NEXT, ARCHBISHOP INNOCENT felt the need to visit Kamchatka again. He hadn't been there for ten years. After traveling down the Amur River to the Tatar Strait, he took a ship going to Sakhalin, Japan, and Kamchatka. While the ship was at anchor in Sakhalin, a gale came up. The ship broke loose and was in great danger from the wind and waves. Everyone was terrified.

In his cabin, the archbishop prayed before the holy icons. He read the prayers that are read before one's death. (He did this so that in case the ship sank, his soul would be prepared for death.) That made him feel calmer and stronger. Then he went up on deck to help the captain.

In the night, the wind drove the ship onto a sandbar, where it broke into pieces. Everyone on board was saved; they only lost the cargo. Archbishop Innocent was the last one off the ship as it was breaking up. On shore, the people and crew knelt with the archbishop to thank God for His mercy. Archbishop Innocent later wrote: "This was my first shipwreck. I've been in great danger before, but never on a ship as it was breaking up. It's certainly not cheery!"

The only ship Archbishop Innocent could find now was one bound for Japan. From there, he would easily be able to find a ship going to Kamchatka. Here we see God's wonderful Providence! Because of the shipwreck, Archbishop Innocent was forced to sail to Japan. There, he was able to help an important person. That person was none other than Father Nicholas Kasatkin, the future Saint Nicholas of Japan.

When Archbishop Innocent met Father Nicholas, the priest was depressed. He had come to Japan eager to teach the people about Jesus Christ and His holy Church. However, the Japanese didn't like people from other countries. The Russians there didn't seem to like him either. Father Nicholas became discouraged. He stayed home and read French and German novels. This was not a good way to be a missionary.

Right away, Archbishop Innocent saw what was needed. "Throw those books away! They're of no use to you here. Study Japanese! Then you'll be able to speak to the people." The archbishop also saw that respect was very important to the Japanese. So it was important for Father Nicholas to look elegant. The archbishop himself sewed Father Nicholas a new cassock of black velvet. He also gave the priest a bronze cross. The archbishop had received this cross as a reward for his work.

This was just what Father Nicholas and the Japanese mission needed. Father Nicholas began to study Japanese. In seven years, he could read and write the language easily. (It's a very difficult language to learn.) He translated the

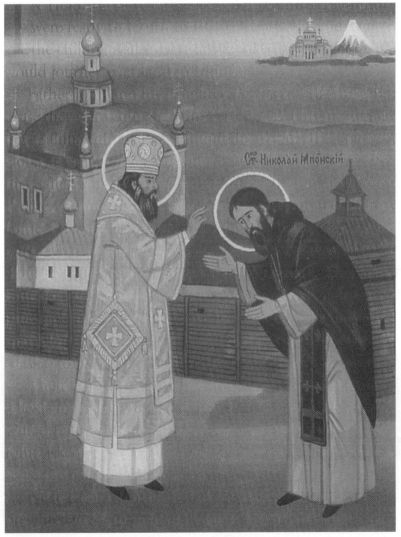

1860. *Archbishop Innocent visits with Saint Nicholas of Japan.*

73

scriptures and church service books into Japanese. He also followed the archbishop's advice and cared for the people's physical health, as well as their spiritual needs. Thanks to Archbishop Innocent, Father Nicholas became a successful missionary. The church in Japan grew in numbers and faith.

As FOR THE ARCHBISHOP, HE FINALLY FOUND a ship that took him to Kamchatka. Twice they were stopped by blizzards, and for two days there was only a little food. This was his fourth trip to that area. Years ago, when he was fifty years old, the trip had taken eight days. Now, at sixty-five, it took him twenty-eight days. One thing was remarkable: his health got better. Many of the pains he had been suffering disappeared during his travels.

A young man named Moshe Silverberg worked as an interpreter on this trip. He was amazed at how difficult the travels and work of the archbishop were. Riding reindeer, eating poor food, living in bad weather, putting up with angry people sometimes, none of this is easy. Yet Archbishop Innocent endured all with patience and good humor. Moshe was amazed. He wrote, "Often, I would talk about his labors to him. He would tell me about the rewards in heaven which await those who do good for God and their neighbor."

Mr. Silverberg, who was young, found he was unable to live the harsh life that the archbishop led at age sixty-five. He returned home. He later wrote of his time with Archbishop Innocent: "Tenderly I kissed the hand of the esteemed old man and boarded my ship. Thus, I was blessed to spend time with a man of rare greatness." Mr. Silverberg later became a Christian, because he was so inspired by the great hierarch.

During this trip, 1,800 natives received baptism. God rewarded the labors of His servant.

12

Spiritual Father of All Russia

IN 1867, RUSSIA SOLD ALASKA to the United States. Archbishop Innocent was pleased. He felt the transfer would help spread the Orthodox faith throughout the United States. To help this come about, he wrote a report to the Synod, making suggestions. These included holding services in English and ordaining Americans into the priesthood. Many of his suggestions were followed.

In November of 1868, Archbishop Innocent received news of the death of his friend, Metropolitan Philaret. Three weeks later, he received an important message from the tsar. His Royal Highness asked the archbishop to come to Moscow immediately. They wanted to make him metropolitan of Moscow. Archbishop Innocent was shocked! He never expected such a thing. (The metropolitan of Moscow was the highest-ranking position in the Russian Church at that time. The metropolitan was thus the spiritual head of the whole Russian Church and her people.) After a day and night in prayer, Archbishop Innocent accepted the new position.

A new bishop was appointed for the Yakutia diocese. Soon, it was time for Archbishop Innocent to leave Yakutsk. The whole city gathered to see him off. One speaker said of Archbishop Innocent that he was "the great apostle of the Word of Christ and spiritual father. You will be remembered all the days of our lives." Tears poured down people's faces. They didn't want to see him go.

Bishop Innocent left Yakutsk on February 15 for Moscow. Father Gabriel, his son, and his oldest grandson traveled with him. As the holy and great archbishop traveled across the Russian land, bells, cheers, and speeches greeted him in every village and monastery. There were dinners, speeches, receptions, and teas in his honor. All Russia knew and loved him. All Russia wanted to greet him, receive his blessing, and wish him well.

The visit to Irkutsk, the hometown of the metropolitan-elect, was very special. As his carriage approached the city, bells from all seventeen church towers rang and rang. The local bishop, clergy, the governor-general, and everyone in the city came to meet him. Archbishop Innocent spent Holy Week, Pascha, and Bright Week in Irkutsk. He stayed at the Monastery of the Ascension. While there, he visited the graves of his parents and wife one last time.

At last, it was time to leave. Archbishop Innocent blessed the abbot, monks, and novices. They wept. Archbishop Innocent dropped to his knees and prayed silently for everyone. Then he arose and bade farewell to his homeland. He knew he would never return.

When they arrived at Kazan, a letter was read to the metropolitan-elect in front of all the people. It was from a person he had entertained as a boy with stories about America. It ended with these words: "Giving you the white cowl with its cross of precious stones, and asking for your prayers, I remain ever favorable toward you." It was signed, Tsar Alexander II. Archbishop Innocent removed his black cowl and placed the white one on his head. The choir sang, "Many Years."

On May 24, 1868, the beloved archbishop arrived in Moscow by train to a tremendous welcome. The train station was crowded with people. All the bells in Moscow rang. Speeches were given and people cheered. The crowd went with him to his residence at the Trinity Apartments.

The following day there were more church services, crowds, and speeches. They started in the Kazan Cathedral. One speaker welcomed the metropolitan-elect with

1868. *Archbishop Innocent is raised to the rank of Metropolitan. The Holy Trinity–St. Sergius Lavra is shown in the background.*

the words, "Blessed is he who comes in the Name of the Lord!"

Then Archbishop Innocent was vested and there was a solemn procession across Red Square to the Dormition Cathedral. There the archbishop gave a speech. One of the things he said was, "How can I, the least of all workers, work in this great and ancient vineyard of Christ?" Attending the service were hundreds of priests, senators, ministers of state, nobles, royalty, and the tsar. They were all dressed in their finest clothes and jewels. It was a great day for Moscow and Russia.

The consecration took place during Divine Liturgy. Our archbishop was now Metropolitan Innocent. With this, he also became the abbot of the Holy Trinity-Saint Sergius Lavra. He was seventy years old.

UP UNTIL THIS TIME, Metropolitan Innocent had served in tiny, poor churches, far away from home. Usually there were only a few native people to sing with him. Now he served in a beautiful cathedral. The icons and paintings were decorated with gold and jewels. Important, rich people came to the services. The choir was large and well-trained. But Metropolitan Innocent's prayers were the same. He did not change when surrounded with riches. He was not changed by becoming an important person. This shows what a godly and humble man he was.

As head of the Russian Church, Metropolitan Innocent held an important position. Many people wanted to see him and ask his help. He received everyone, even those who weren't so important in some people's eyes. (Not every metropolitan did this.) When people found out about this, even more people came. Often there would be three hundred a week. He gave advice to people and prayed for them. Sometimes he gave money from his own pocket to those in need. Everyone who visited him received help. The people grew to love, respect, and trust him.

As the abbot of the Holy Trinity-Saint Sergius Lavra, Metropolitan Innocent had work to do there, also. There was a seminary there, of which he was also head. On his first visit to the Lavra, he spoke to each monk and seminary student. He said that though he had been a monk for twenty-five years, he had much to learn from the youngest novice. He climbed the ladders up to the student bedrooms. He listened to their lessons. They remembered his humble manner and fatherly love for a long time.

Another of Metropolitan Innocent's duties was to serve as a member of the Holy Synod. The Synod met in Saint Petersburg. This was a long journey for a busy metropolitan. Our metropolitan began to live in Saint Petersburg in the winter and spring. Then he lived in Moscow in the summer and fall. This saved him a lot of travel time.

While staying in Saint Petersburg, Metropolitan Innocent once traveled to the city of Kronstadt. There he visited

1870.
Metropolitan Innocent travels to Kronstadt, where he meets Saint John of Kronstadt.

Father John Sergieff. Father John was also a missionary. (The Church glorified Father John Sergieff in 1964. We know him as Saint John of Kronstadt.) The two men became close friends. They inspired and encouraged each other.

Most of all, Metropolitan Innocent brought new life to the Church in Moscow. He started a department of iconography. He inspired people about their faith. He encouraged them to attend church, fast, and pray. He also corrected people who had wrong ideas about the Faith. All the people began to live more as Christians and to serve God with love. The whole Church and its people were blessed by this man of God.

13

Life at the Capital

IT WOULD SEEM THAT LIFE IN MOSCOW would have been easier for Metropolitan Innocent, who was getting old. It wasn't as cold. Travel was much easier and he didn't have to go so far. He had a large staff to help him. There was always enough food. In many ways, it *was* easier. But Metropolitan Innocent found life in Moscow difficult. He didn't like the big city as much as the country. He said he always felt healthier in the fresh air.

The solution was a summer home. (The Russians call this a *dacha*. Even people without much money often have a dacha.) Metropolitan Innocent designed one for himself. It was built in a wooded area in Cherkizovo. This was close enough to the city for the metropolitan to continue his work. There was a chapel in the house, where he was able to pray and hold services. This home made life easier for the metropolitan. After all, he had lived outdoors most of his life.

Another difficult thing for Metropolitan Innocent was his health. He had pains in his legs, and his eyes were bad. He told one visitor, "There are some good days when I can see some things, but it never lasts long. Mostly I see everything in a fog." Doctors operated on the eye, but it didn't help. One eye became blind. Of all his troubles, this was the hardest on him. He hated the idea of going blind. His son, Father Gabriel, wrote, "It is very painful, very sad, that Papa will never again see with the eye. Let us run to the Lord with all our soul and heart. There is no longer any hope in the doctors."

The metropolitan thought he should retire. The tsar disagreed. Such love, faith, and zeal would not be easily found in another man. Instead, they gave him more people to help him with his work. He served the church services and said the long prayers from memory.

During the last two weeks of Great Lent, Metropolitan Innocent spent his time in church or in prayer. At home, he had his grandchildren read him the Gospels or lives of the saints out loud. He kept a strict fast and gave money to the poor. In this way, he fed his soul and prepared for death.

Not far from Moscow was the monastery of Optina. This great monastery was famous throughout Holy Russia. Its spiritual life was of the highest quality. Also, the Optina elders were famous throughout all Russia and beyond. These men were very close to God and worked miracles. They could read men's souls like a book. They knew what spiritual medicines to apply to men's spiritual sicknesses. People came from everywhere to see the elders and get their advice or help.

The most famous of the elders was Elder Ambrose. He served the monastery and the Russian people for over forty years. The elder was meek, wise, and full of love. The most hardhearted people were brought to love of God through his prayers. The most difficult problems were solved by his prayerful help.

In 1871, Metropolitan Innocent traveled to Optina to visit Elder Ambrose. The elder was sick and old at this time. He spent most of his time in his cell. After the metropolitan visited the church and venerated the icons, he said, "Well, now let's go to see the elder." He turned around and there was Elder Ambrose in front of him. The metropolitan was surprised. He knew how sick the elder was. He said, "Why did you take the trouble to come here? I myself will come to you."

1871. *Metropolitan Innocent visits with Elder Ambrose at Optina Monastery. You can see a little of what Optina looks like, through the window.*

When the metropolitan arrived at Elder Ambrose's cell, he saw pictures of Metropolitan Philaret and himself on the walls. The two men talked a long time. Metropolitan Innocent came to love and respect Elder Ambrose. As he left, he said, "A grace-filled elder!"

IN SPITE OF HIS POOR HEALTH, the metropolitan was a very busy man. He got up at four o'clock in the morning and went to Divine Liturgy. At nine o'clock, he began work. He rested a little in the afternoon, then worked until nine at night. Besides taking care of church work, he listened to his grandchildren's lessons. Sometimes his family read him the newspaper or a book in the evening. He was very grateful to have members of his family close by. They were a close family and helped each other in everything.

1872.
Emperor Alexander II awards Metropolitan Innocent the St. Andrew medal.

When the metropolitan wished to see his new diocese, his method of travel was different from before. Instead of riding a reindeer or bull, or taking a dogsled or kayak, he rode in a beautiful horse-drawn carriage. He found he didn't like it as much. He liked the simple life in America and Siberia better. "Somehow I felt healthy there. Fresh air is a great thing."

In spite of his age and poor health, Metropolitan Innocent did many good things in Moscow. He made sure the priests' widows and orphans were cared for. He built a house for the poor. It sat on 106 acres of land and was a blessing to many people.

For Metropolitan Innocent's many, many labors, Tsar Alexander II gave him the Saint Andrew the First-Called Medal in 1872. This was a great honor. With it, the tsar thanked the metropolitan for his service to the Church and his country.

PERHAPS METROPOLITAN Innocent's greatest success in Moscow was the Orthodox Missionary Society. Missionary work was always close to Metropolitan Innocent's heart. As he prayed for the Russian people, he came to believe that everyone should help with missionary work. He decided to start an organization that anyone, rich or poor, could join. He would ask all of Russia to help in the missionary work of the Church.

Metropolitan Innocent called a meeting. He himself wrote to all the important people in Moscow, asking them to come. Hundreds of people *did* come. There were so many they couldn't all fit in the meeting room.

At this first meeting, the metropolitan gave a speech.

He talked about the importance of missionary work. He also said that hard work alone would not mean they would be successful. Why not? Because people come to truth and the right faith only through the power of God. "No one can come to Me unless the Father who sent Me draws him" (John 6:44). Everyone was inspired by his words. Thus, the Orthodox Missionary Society began.

1876. *Metropolitan Innocent consecrates the altar of Christ the Savior Cathedral in Moscow.*

The society was a great success. It did much good, bringing people to the Holy Orthodox Church in Siberia, America, and Japan. People all over Russia prayed, sewed church linens and vestments, and raised money. The society lasted until the 1920s, a few years after the terrible Revolution of 1917.

Metropolitan Innocent also consecrated the altar of Christ the Savior Cathedral. The construction of this cathedral had been begun in 1813. It was built to mark Russia's victory over Napoleon and would not be completed until 1883. However, the consecration allowed church services to be held while the work was being finished.

14

The Final Journey

IN EARLY 1878, METROPOLITAN INNOCENT grew weaker. The fast of Great Lent weakened him even more. However, as summer came, he grew stronger. He especially enjoyed walks in the woods at his dacha that year. He even picked up his full workload. His son, Father Gabriel, saw how well his father was doing. Father Gabriel said, "Oh! If only it were not for his eyes—which now see almost nothing—he'd be like an eagle! But may God's will be done."

This burst of strength didn't last long, however. In the fall, Metropolitan Innocent was unable to travel to Saint Petersburg for the Holy Synod. By January of 1879, he

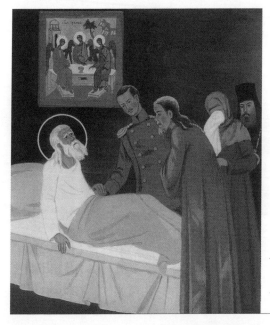

1879.
Metropolitan Innocent becomes very sick.

couldn't stand for very long. He became dizzy often. The metropolitan still wanted to keep up with his church work. "Business takes my mind off my sickness." His family and staff told him not to think about work. He would mutter, "But I'm bored." The metropolitan gave a large amount of money to the church in the village of Anga where he grew up. He went to church every day and spent much time in prayer, preparing his soul for death.

On Holy Monday (March 25), Metropolitan Innocent asked that the Iberian icon of the Theotokos be brought. His staff helped him kneel before the icon, as he wished. He prayed with all his heart, though he could not see it. Then he kissed it, with tears. He seemed better after this. That evening the metropolitan made his last confession. The Canon for the Departure of the Soul was read for the first time.

On Holy Tuesday Metropolitan Innocent received the Sacrament of Healing. He blessed the thirty people who came to pray with him and for him.

On Holy Wednesday, the metropolitan asked them to celebrate the Divine Liturgy early, at 2:00 A.M. They were to bring him the Holy Gifts immediately. Metropolitan Innocent received the Gifts standing by himself and fully vested.

During the Lamentation Service of Holy and Great Friday, the metropolitan asked to have the Canon of the Departure of the Soul read a second and then a third time. After the Sacrament of Healing, he said goodbye to his family and household, and blessed everyone.

Early in the morning of Holy and Great Saturday, the beloved hierarch died, at 2:45 A.M. He was eighty-one years

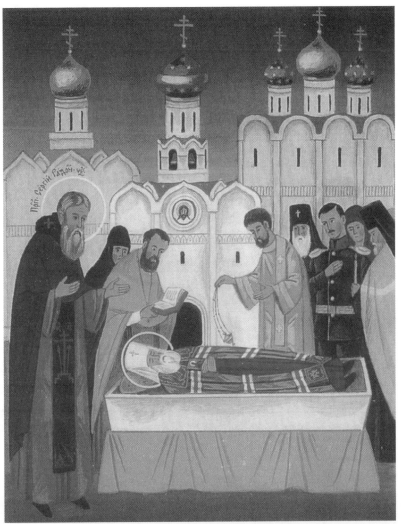

1879. *Metropolitan Innocent is buried at the Holy Trinity–St. Sergius Lavra. Saint Sergius (who died in 1392) is shown on the left, as if visibly present, honoring the abbot of his monastery, and welcoming him into the heavenly kingdom.*

old. At eleven o'clock that morning, the great Ivan the Terrible Bell in the Kremlin rang very slowly. All Moscow stopped and listened. They understood it meant the death of their spiritual father.

For two days, people came to the Trinity Apartments

to say goodbye. Thousands upon thousands came for the funeral. All of Moscow and much of Russia mourned while singing, "Christ is risen."

BEFORE HIS DEATH, METROPOLITAN Innocent had told his family what he wanted for his funeral. Because he was humble, he said, "Do not allow any speeches at my burial; there is too much praise in these. Instead, preach a sermon over me, for this can teach the people. Here is the Bible verse for you to use, 'The Lord guides a man safely in the way he should go.'" (Psalm 37:23)

After the Paschal Divine Liturgy on Bright Thursday, Metropolitan Innocent was buried at the Holy Trinity-St. Sergius Lavra, next to his friend, Metropolitan Philaret.

15

His Glorification

ON OCTOBER 6, 1977, the holy Orthodox Church glorified Metropolitan Innocent as a saint. He is honored as one of her greatest missionaries.

Saint Innocent of Alaska is honored as a saint even outside the Orthodox Church. Other Christians and even some Moslem people ask for his prayers. His great-great-grandson, Archimandrite Innokenty Veniaminov, has said that Tatars, Azerbaijanis, Chechens, and Jews ask him to pray to Saint Innocent, so that he will help them.

Through his work and prayers, before and after death, Saint Innocent has brought America and Russia together in the Orthodox faith. He hears our prayers and brings them before God, who is merciful to all.

IN THE BEAUTIFUL LIFE of Saint Innocent, we can learn many things. We see God's love for all people and all time. God prepared the Aleut people to receive the holy Gospel. Then He sent Saint Innocent to teach them. We see what great good one man can do, with God's help and grace. We see how people can inspire one another and help each other on the path to the Kingdom of heaven. We see the qualities of a godly man in Saint Innocent. And we learn that one of the straightest paths to heaven is by serving our neighbor.

May you who read this be inspired by this life and find the Kingdom of heaven. Holy Saint Innocent, pray to God for us!

Troparion to Saint Innocent of Alaska
Tone 3

O, paramount messenger to peoples
of distant lands held in pagan ignorance,
you enlightened their path to salvation
and labored as an apostle to the Far East,
from Siberia to Alaska and America.
O holy Hierarch Innocent,
pray to the Lord of all
to grant peace to the world
and to our souls great mercy.

1977.
In heaven, Saint Innocent has united America to Russia in the Orthodox faith and is an intercessor for all who pray to him.

GLOSSARY

abbot: The spiritual father and superior of a monastery.

Annunciation: The feast of the Church that celebrates the appearance of the Archangel Gabriel to the Virgin Mary. He told her she was going to have a child, Jesus, by the Holy Spirit and that the One born of her would be the Son of God (Luke 1:26–33).

apostolic: In the spirit of the Twelve Apostles.

archbishop: A high-ranking bishop who rules over an important diocese or more than one diocese.

archimandrite: A hieromonk (monk-priest) who usually is in charge of one or more monasteries; or an abbot in priestly rank; or sometimes just a title of honor for a hieromonk.

archpriest: A title of honor given to a priest in recognition of his service.

bishop: The highest rank of the priesthood. One who rules a diocese; he rules over an area of churches, missions, and monasteries. He must be a monk first. (In the Orthodox Church, a priest may either be married or be a monk, but a bishop must be a monk.)

Bright Week: The week following Pascha; Monday of that week is Bright Monday, Tuesday is Bright Tuesday, etc.

canon: A set of verses and hymns sung to a saint, for a feast, or for some special need. It uses themes from the Old Testament and is usually sung at Matins.

cassock: A long, black robe worn by clergy and monastics.

cathedral: The church that serves as a bishop's seat.

cell: A room or dwelling place where a monastic lives.

chrismate/chrismation: The sacrament of sealing with chrism, giving the gift of the Holy Spirit to those who are baptized. Chrism is prepared by the patriarch or head of the Church.

"Christ is risen": This phrase is sung many times during the Pascha services, and in church services from Pascha until Pentecost.

("Christ is risen from the dead, trampling down death by death, and upon those in the tombs bestowing life.") The first three words are also used as a greeting between Orthodox Christians. The response is, "Indeed He is risen."

clergy: An ordained person. Originally, this could be a reader, subdeacon, deacon, priest, and so forth. Now it usually refers only to deacons, priests, and bishops.

commemorate: To honor the memory of someone or something.

consecrate: To set apart and dedicate to the service and worship of God.

cowl: See *white cowl.*

deacon: A man ordained to assist the priest.

diocesan see: The place where the bishop's residence and offices are located.

diocese: An area of churches, missions, monasteries, and people ruled by one bishop.

Divine Liturgy: A sacrament of the Orthodox Church in which bread and wine are consecrated to become the Body and Blood of Christ, and at which the faithful partake of these Holy Gifts.

elder: A spiritual father and guide to a number of monastics and people, who is filled with the grace of the Holy Spirit.

epistle: A reading from the New Testament, not one of the four Gospels.

faithful, the: Those who believe and confess the Orthodox faith (especially faith in Jesus Christ as the Son of God, the Holy Trinity, and the Virgin Birth); the people of God.

fast: To abstain from eating certain foods. In the Orthodox Church, the faithful fast on Wednesdays and Fridays. Monastics also fast on Mondays. On fast days they don't eat meat, fish, oil, or wine. Also on fast days, one eats in moderation. There are other special fast days and periods of fasting during the year.

feast/feastday: A holy day. Every Sunday is a feastday, because we commemorate the Resurrection on that day. Other feastdays commemorate events in the life of our Lord, the Theotokos, the saints, and so forth. These days are usually observed by a Vigil and Divine Liturgy.

First Hour: One of the daily church services, originally sung at six o'clock in the morning. It commemorates Christ being given to the Gentiles and brought before Pilate.

glorify/glorification: The formal statement by the bishops of a local Orthodox church that a certain holy man or woman is a saint and is to be venerated and honored as someone who can pray for us in heaven, before the Throne of God. A service is composed, which may be sung on the feastday of that saint every year. (Known as *canonize* or *canonization* in the Western churches.)

Great Lent: The great forty-day fast that comes before Pascha (known as Easter in the Western churches).

hierarch: A bishop, archbishop, metropolitan, or patriarch.

Holy Gifts: The Body and Blood of Christ.

Holy Synod: A group of bishops gathered together in council. During the period when there was no patriarch in Russia, the Church in Russia was ruled by the Holy Synod (or Synod) and the tsar.

icon: A holy picture of our Lord Jesus Christ, the Theotokos, a feast, or a saint, painted in a traditional manner and style, used in prayer and worship. An icon is a "window" into heaven, because it represents something of heaven, rather than something in this world, and because the honor given to the icon passes to the person portrayed.

iconography: The art of painting icons.

iconostasis: A partition between the altar and the main part of the church on which holy icons are placed in a specific manner.

lavra: A large monastery, often made up of many monasteries, sketes, and hermitages.

"Many Years": A song sung by the faithful for their ruling bishop, wishing him a healthy life of many years.

Matins: One of the daily church services which takes place at night or early in the morning. The service consists of psalms and canons. It celebrates the birth of God and offers thanks and praise to Him.

metropolitan: A bishop who rules over many dioceses, bishops, and archbishops. He is often the head of a local church. When there was no patriarch in Russia, the metropolitan of Moscow was the highest-ranking clergyman in Russia and Russia's spiritual head.

metropolitan-elect: A bishop or person who has been appointed to be metropolitan but has not yet been consecrated.

moleben: A prayer service where the faithful ask for heavenly help or give thanks to God. Someone would ask for a moleben at a time of special need or a time of special thanksgiving.

monastery: A place where monks or nuns live.

monastic (monk, nun): A person who gives vows of poverty, chastity, and obedience before his superior and God. A monastic lives a consecrated life of prayer and labor and does not marry. Because monastics don't marry and spend much time in prayer, their life is called "angelic." There are no separate orders of monastics in Eastern Orthodoxy as there are in the Catholic Church.

Nativity: The feast of the Birth of Christ (known as Christmas in the Western churches).

New Martyrs: Martyrs of the Church in recent times, especially those suffering under the Moslems or communists.

novice: One who is taking the first step in the monastic life.

ordination: The setting apart for liturgical service of priests and deacons. Ordination is a sacrament performed by a bishop.

pannikhida: A prayer service for someone who has died.

parish: The group of people under the spiritual care of one priest.

Pascha: The feast of the Resurrection of our Lord Jesus Christ (known as Easter in the Western churches).

patriarch: A bishop selected by his fellow bishops to rule over their national church.

patron saint: When a person is baptized in the Orthodox Church, he or she is given the name of a saint. This saint becomes the person's heavenly helper, who watches over him or her.

pectoral cross: A special cross worn by bishops, archimandrites, and certain priests, as allowed by the bishop or archbishop.

phelonion: A long, large capelike vestment worn by a priest over his other vestments.

pilgrimage: A journey to a holy place or places to seek divine help and blessing.

priest: A man who, through ordination by a bishop, has received divine authority and strength to serve the sacraments and carry out the saving work of Christ. In the Orthodox Church, a man must either marry or become a monk before he can be ordained a priest. A married priest would usually serve in a parish. A hieromonk (monk-priest) would normally serve in a monastery.

Providence (Divine Providence): God's divine guidance or care.

relics: The grace-filled body of a saint, or pieces of bone or objects associated with a saint or holy person, which are venerated by the faithful.

sacrament (mystery): A sacred ceremony, performed by a priest, in which visible things communicate to the soul of the faithful the invisible grace of God.

seminary: A school where clergy are taught and trained.

sign of the cross (to cross oneself): Orthodox make the sign of the cross by holding the hand with the thumb, forefinger, and index fingers held together (as a symbol of the Trinity), with the other two fingers against the palm, and touching the forehead, chest, right shoulder, and then left shoulder, in recognition that every power of mind, heart, soul, and strength are for the service of God. This is also a way of protecting oneself from evil. (This is different from the way Catholics cross themselves.)

synaxis: A gathering of many together, such as a gathering of saints.

Theotokos: A Greek word meaning, "the Birth-giver of God." This name is given to Mary, who gave birth to Jesus Christ and who was a virgin before, during, and after childbirth.

tonsure: The church service in which a novice is clothed in the monastic clothing and makes formal vows before God and his or her superior, thus becoming a monk or nun.

troparion: A short hymn in honor of a saint or feast, which contains its meaning.

tsar: The emperor or king of pre-revolutionary Russia. (The origin of the word is *Caesar*.)

tsarevich: The oldest son of the tsar, who will be the next tsar.

venerate: To give special honor to something that is holy.

vested: Dressed in the vestments of one's rank.

vestments: The special clothing worn by clergy during church services.

Vigil: The service sung on the eve of a feast, consisting of Vespers, Matins, and the First Hour.

white cowl: The special headcovering worn by the patriarch. This was also worn by the metropolitan of Moscow during the time when there was no patriarch in Russia.

Your Eminence: The proper way to address an archbishop or metropolitan.

Your Grace: The proper way to address a bishop.

yurt: A collapsible tent used by the nomads of Central Asia, somewhat resembling a wigwam.

Also by Conciliar Press . . .

Ella's Story: The Duchess Who Became a Saint
by Maria Tobias, with illustrations by Bonnie Gillis

Ella's Story brings to life the amazing journey of Princess Elizabeth, from privileged childhood to eventual martyrdom. While her biography, as St. Elizabeth the New Martyr, is available to adults, this is the first such book for girls, written in an approachable, appealing style. Maria Tobias tells the Princess' story in such a lively way that the book is hard to put down. Elizabeth, a real princess, is gifted with all those qualities girls still seek (intelligence, beauty, wealth, renown), converts to Orthodoxy, and subsequently sheds all earthly glory for the greater prize of the martyr's crown. She is a true role model for today. **A chapter book, with black-and-white illustrations.**
• Paperback, 80 pages (ISBN 1-888212-70-5) Order No. 006536—$8.95*

The Wonderful Life of Russia's Saint, Sergius of Radonezh
by Alvin Alexsi Currier, illustrated by Nadja Glazunova

Bartholomew was a little boy who loved nature, his family, and God. But he was sad because he couldn't read. One day he went into a forest and found a holy monk who gave him some blessed bread and prayed for him to read . . . and he did! Bartholomew later became the monk Sergius, and soon grew into a holy man who performed many miracles. Read about the life of St. Sergius from the age of 7 until his repose several miracles later. Well-written and beautifully illustrated. **Picture book for ages 4 to 11.**
• Hardcover, 40 pages (ISBN 1-888212-24-1) Order No. 005131—$17.95*

The Abbot and I (As told by Josie the Cat)
by Sarah Cowie, illustrated by Sarah Selby

Josie the cat has a special relationship with a monastery. She is the abbot's cat. Visit with Josie as she guides children on a special tour of a monastery: having tea with the the abbot in his cell, watching monks garden and sew, and taking part in an all-night vigil. **Picturebook for preschool and up.**
• Paperback, 24 pages (ISBN 1-888212-25-X) Order No. 005197—$8.95*

The Monk Who Grew Prayer
written and illustrated by Claire Brandenburg

A monk prays deep in the forest. It looks like he is doing just simple, ordinary tasks, such as chopping wood and tending to his garden. But as he works he is really growing prayer. The monk prays continually throughout the day and night, and, as the seasons pass, he becomes a holy man. This delightful, beautifully illustrated book teaches children that no matter what they are doing, or what hour of the day it is, they too can pray. **Picturebook for preschool and up.**
• Paperback, 32 pages (ISBN 1-888212-66-7) Order No. 006177—$9.95*

*plus applicable tax and postage & handling charges.
Please call Conciliar Press at 800-967-7377 for complete ordering information.